This Walker book belongs to:

_____

_____

_____

La La La

KATE DiCAMILLO

A story of hope illustrated by

JAIME KIM

WALKER BOOKS
AND SUBSIDIARIES

LONDON · BOSTON · SYDNEY · AUCKLAND

La

La   La   La

La

La

Laaaaaaaaa!

La La La La La La La

La

La La

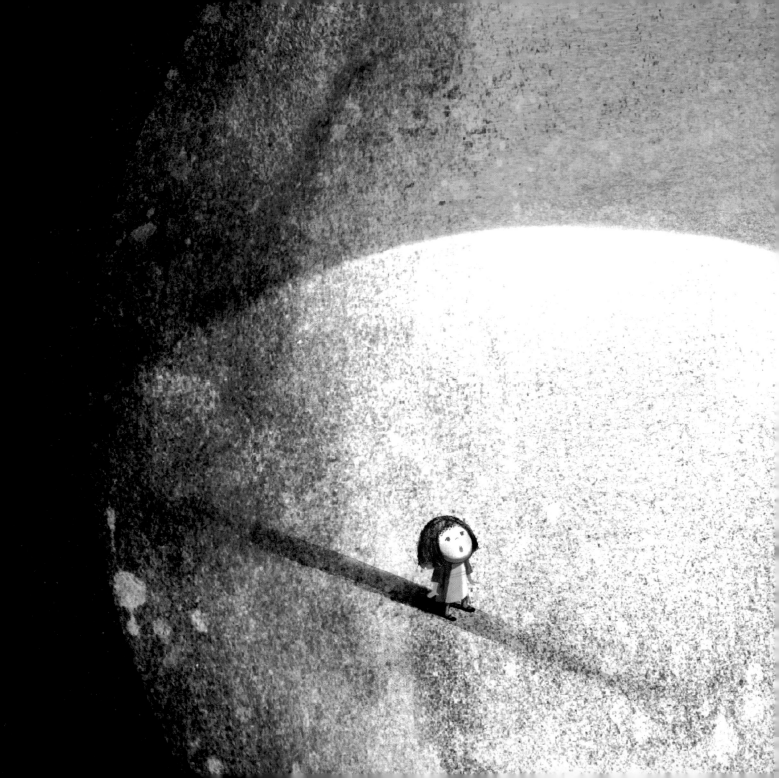

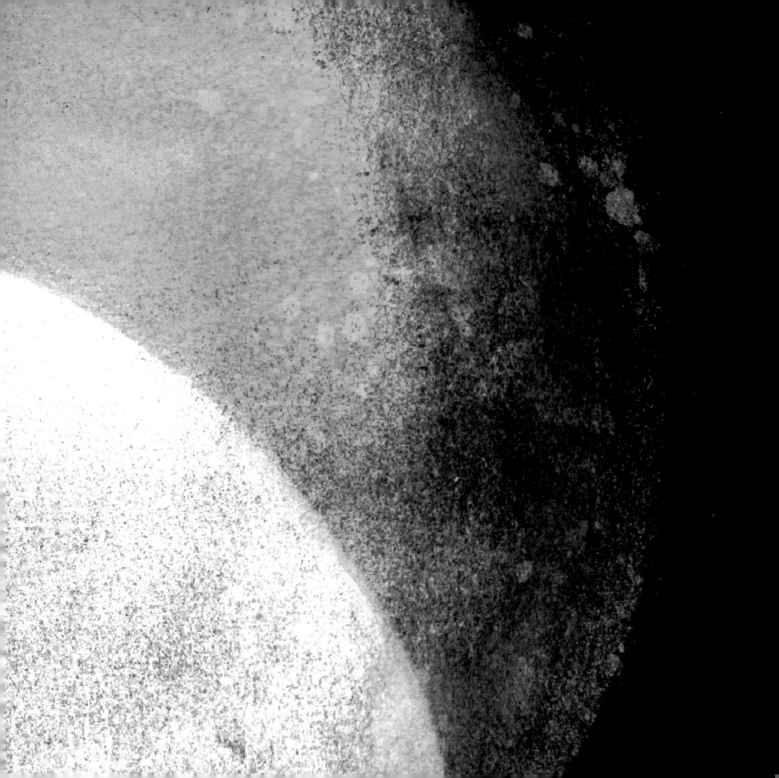

zzz...

La

La
La
La

La La La

This story started with my sketching a very small, very
lonely, very uncertain circle. And then a big circle appeared
way up high above the small circle. The little circle was
utterly charmed by the big circle — but it was so far away!
How could they connect?

I played with those circles for a long time.

Finally, I figured that what the small circle needed to do was
sing. Because even if we are small and alone and afraid, if we
sing, sometimes someone answers us back.

And look! I was right! Because here is Jaime Kim's beautiful
art answering my small, tentative song.

— Kate DiCamillo

Just like the girl in this book, I also had a time during my childhood when I felt lonely. Because of my timid and quiet nature, I had few friends and found it difficult to step outside of my own private world. Then one day my little sister was born. I still remember when my mom let me hold her for the first time. It was an unforgettable moment. While I was illustrating this story, I thought of that memory and tried to capture the relief, the overwhelming emotion, and the joy of finding the most precious friend in the world. I completed each illustration with the sincere wish that the little girl in the story would no longer be lonely. I hope all of those who read this book will find their way out of loneliness too, just like me and the little girl. I dedicate this book to my little sister, Soma, who will always be a lifelong friend of mine.

— Jaime Kim

For Karen Lotz, who believes in the song
K. D.

For my little sister, Soma
J. K.

First published 2017 by Walker Books Ltd
87 Vauxhall Walk, London SE11 5HJ

This edition published 2018

2 4 6 8 10 9 7 5 3 1

Text © 2017 Kate DiCamillo
Illustrations © 2017 Jaime Kim

The right of Kate DiCamillo and Jaime Kim to be identified as the author and illustrator respectively of
this work has been asserted by them in accordance with the Copyright, Designs and Patents Act 1988

This book has been typeset in Caflisch Script Pro

Printed in China

British Library Cataloguing in Publication Data: a catalogue record
for this book is available from the British Library

ISBN 978-1-4063-7988-4

www.walker.co.uk